This book belongs to:

....

....

....

Retold by Gaby Goldsack
Illustrated by Ruth Galloway (Advocate)
Designed by Jester Designs

Language consultant: Betty Root

ISBN 0-75259-429-X

This is a P³ book
This edition published 2002 ·

P³
Queen Street House
4 Queen Street
Bath BA1 1HE, UK

Copyright © Exclusive Editions 2002

Printed in China.

p^3

Hansel
and
Gretel

Helping your Child Read

Learning to read is an exciting challenge for most children. From a very early age, sharing story books with children, talking about the pictures, and guessing what might happen next are all very important parts of the reading experience.

Sharing reading

Set aside a regular quiet time to share reading with younger children, or to be on hand to encourage older children as they develop into independent readers.

First Readers are intended to encourage and support the early stages of learning to read. They present well-loved tales that children will enjoy hearing again and again. Familiarity helps children to identify some of the words and phrases.

When you feel your child is ready to move ahead, encourage him or her to join in so that you read the story aloud together. Always pause to talk about the pictures. The easy-to-read speech bubbles in **First Readers** provide an excellent "joining-in" activity. The bright, clear illustrations and matching text will help children to understand the story.

Building confidence

In time, children will want to read *to* you. When this happens, be patient and give continual praise. They may not read all the words correctly, but children's substitutions are often very good guesses.

The repetition in each book is particularly helpful for building confidence. If your child cannot read a particular word, go back to the beginning of the sentence and read it together so the meaning is not lost. Most importantly, do not continue if your child is tired or just needs a change.

Reading alone

The next step is to ask your child to read alone. Try to be available to give help and support. Remember to give lots of encouragement and praise.

Together with other simple stories, **First Readers** will help ensure reading is an enjoyable and rewarding experience.

Once upon a time there was a boy
called Hansel and a girl called Gretel.
They lived with their father and
stepmother near a dark woods.
Their father was a poor woodcutter.

One day, there was no food to eat.
They were all hungry.

That night Hansel
and Gretel heard their
father and
stepmother talking.

There's no
food to eat.

"There's no food to eat," said
the woodcutter.
"Take Hansel and Gretel to the dark
woods and leave them there," said
the stepmother.

Leave Hansel
and Gretel in
the woods.

Gretel was scared.
Hansel had a plan.

He went outside and
got some pebbles.

12

The next day the woodcutter took
Hansel and Gretel into the dark woods.

As they walked Hansel dropped
the pebbles.

They walked deep into the dark woods.

"Stay here," said the woodcutter.
"I will come back."

The woodcutter did not come back.

Gretel was scared.

"Don't be scared," said Hansel.

"We can follow the pebbles home."

Hansel and Gretel followed the pebbles. They were soon home.

The woodcutter was happy to see them. The stepmother was not.

We'll soon be home.

"Take them into the dark woods again," said the stepmother.

Hansel went to get some pebbles. The door was locked so he got some bread crumbs.

The woodcutter took Hansel and Gretel
to the dark woods.

As they walked Hansel dropped
the bread crumbs.

They walked deep into the dark woods.
"Stay here," said the woodcutter.
"I will come back."

The woodcutter did not come back.
Gretel was scared.

"Don't be scared," said Hansel.
"We can follow the bread crumbs."

But the birds ate the bread crumbs.
Hansel and Gretel could not find their
way home.

Hansel and Gretel were lost in
the dark wood.

They walked until they saw a house.

The house was made of candy and
cookies.

Hansel and Gretel were hungry.

They began to eat the house.

An old woman came out of the house.

"Come in," she said.

The old woman was a witch.
She locked Hansel in a cage.
She made Gretel feed Hansel.
She wanted Hansel to be fat
enough to eat.

Every day the witch went to Hansel.

"Hold out your finger!" she said.

Hansel held out a thin chicken bone.

The witch could not see well.

"You're not fat enough!" said the witch.

Not fat enough!

One day, the witch could wait no longer.
She made Gretel heat the water in the
big pot.

The witch looked into the big pot
to check if the water was hot.
Gretel pushed her in.

25

Gretel unlocked the cage.

Hansel and Gretel ran away.

They ran and ran all the way home.

Their father was happy to see them.

The stepmother had gone away.

They all lived happily ever after.

Read and Say

How many of these words can you say? The pictures will help you. Look back in your book and see if you can find the words in the story.

woods

door

woodcutter

pebbles

chicken bone

bread crumbs

cage

witch

stepmother

pot

29

Titles in this series:

Chicken-Licken
Cinderella
The Gingerbread Man
Hansel and Gretel
The Three Billy Goats Gruff
The Ugly Duckling